Amphibians

BY MICHELLE LEVINE

amicus
high interest

Amicus High Interest is an imprint of Amicus
P.O. Box 1329, Mankato, MN 56002
www.amicuspublishing.us

Library of Congress Cataloging-in-Publication Data
Levine, Michelle.
 Amphibians / Michelle Levine.
    pages cm. — (Animal kingdom)
 Includes bibliographical references and index.
 Summary: "An introduction to what characteristics animals
in the amphibian animal class have and how they fit into the
animal kingdom"— Provided by publisher.
 Audience: Grades: K to grade 3.
 ISBN 978-1-60753-471-6 (library binding) —
 ISBN 978-1-60753-618-5 (e-book)
1. Amphibians—Juvenile literature. I. Title.
 QL644.2.L478 2015
 597.8—dc23
                                         2013031404

Editor: Wendy Dieker
Series Designer: Kathleen Petelinsek
Book Designer: Heather Dreisbach
Photo Researcher: Kurtis Kinneman

Photo Credits:
NHPA/SuperStock, cover; Minden Pictures/SuperStock, 5;
Michael & Patricia Fogden/CORBIS, 6; asturianu/123rf, 8–9;
Tierfotoagentur/Alamy, 10; Maximilian Weinzierl/Alamy, 13;
FloridaStock/Shutterstock, 14; Helen Hotson/Shutterstock,
17; Dirk Ercken/Shutterstock, 18; E.R. Degginger/Alamy,
21; cbstockfoto/Alamy, 22; Danita Delimont/Alamy, 25;
Maximilian Weinzierl/Alamy, 26; kajornyot/Shutterstock, 29

Printed in the United States of America at Corporate Graphics
in North Mankato, Minnesota.

10 9 8 7 6 5 4 3 2 1

Table of Contents

What Is an Amphibian?

Splash! A frog jumps into a pond. Croak! A toad calls out to another toad. Nearby, a salamander crawls in the woods. And a newt creeps over leaves. How are these animals alike? They belong to the same animal class. They are all amphibians.

Frogs are amphibians. They live on land and in water.

A caecilian (seh-SILL-yun) lives underground. Some of them grow as large as snakes!

 How many kinds of amphibians are there?

Amphibian means "double life." That's because most amphibians live two lives. They begin life in water. Then they move to land.

These animals are alike in other ways. They all have a backbone. And they have smooth, thin skin. Frogs and toads are common amphibians. So are salamanders. Caecilians look like big worms. But they are amphibians too.

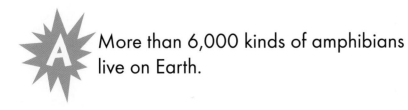

More than 6,000 kinds of amphibians live on Earth.

The skin of an amphibian is special. It helps the animal breathe. You breathe with your lungs. So do some amphibians. But they mostly take in air through their skin. No other animal does this.

Amphibians also use their skin to get water. You drink with your mouth. Not amphibians. Their skin soaks in water.

Salamander skin helps take in air and water.

A tree frog warms itself in the sun.

All amphibians are **cold-blooded**. Their bodies match the temperature around them. You are warm-blooded. Your body temperature stays the same. It does not change in the heat or cold.

Amphibians **bask** to warm up. They lay out in the sun. They soak up its heat. They find shady places to cool down.

Eat or Be Eaten

Zoom! An amphibian's tongue zips out. It catches its **prey**. Crunch! Its strong jaws bite down. Its sharp teeth chew the prey.

Amphibians are **carnivores**. They eat other animals. Amphibians eat bugs, worms, and snails. Bigger amphibians also eat birds and mice. Some even eat other amphibians!

An earthworm makes a good meal for this amphibian. Yum!

**Birds that live near water
eat frogs and toads.**

 Why are some amphibians so colorful?

Amphibians must watch out for **predators**. Ducks and small water animals eat baby amphibians. Larger animals, such as raccoons, eat adult amphibians.

How do amphibians stay safe? Many of them taste bad. Their bodies make poison that comes out of their skin. It can make predators sick. So they keep away. Amphibians also run or jump away from predators.

The bright color sends a message to predators. It says, "Danger! I'm poisonous!" Eating them can be deadly.

Living on Land and in Water

Some adult amphibians live in water. But most live on land. Amphibians like damp places. They live in woods or rain forests. They also live near rivers, streams, and ponds. But amphibians can live almost anywhere. Some live in dry grasslands. Others live in icy places. They even live in the desert!

 Do any amphibians live in the sea?

A stream in the woods is a good home for an amphibian.

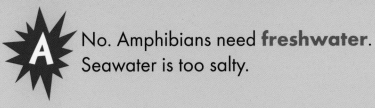

A No. Amphibians need **freshwater**. Seawater is too salty.

**This horned toad lives
in a wet rain forest.**

 What is the difference between
frogs and toads?

Amphibians like damp places for a reason. Their skin must stay moist. Dry skin cannot soak in air or water. An amphibian with dry skin can die. So amphibians make **mucus**. This thick liquid coats their skin. Amphibians also rest under wet leaves. They stay inside damp, rotting logs. And they live underground. They come out when it rains.

 Toads belong to the frog family. Toads have fat bodies and bumpy skin. Frogs are slimmer. And they have smoother skin.

Making Babies

Most amphibians go to water to **mate**.
Male frogs and toads call out to females.
Their song says, "Let's get together!"
Then the female lays her eggs. Some
amphibians lay a few eggs at a time.
Others lay thousands. The bullfrog lays
up to 80,000 eggs at a time!

Salamander babies will soon hatch from these eggs.

Tree frog tadpoles live
underwater until they are adults.

Most amphibian babies hatch out of eggs. Amphibian babies are called **larvae** or tadpoles. Frog and toad larvae look like fish. They have a tail and no legs. They have **gills** too. The gills let them breathe underwater. Salamander larvae also have gills and tails. Most are born with tiny legs too.

Some amphibians are larvae for only a few weeks. Others stay larvae for months or years. Then something amazing happens. Their bodies start to change. Frog and toad larvae grow legs. Their tail goes away. So do their gills. Most salamanders also lose their gills. But they keep their tail. Most grown amphibians leave the water. They start living on land.

 Are all amphibians born in water?

**These young newts
live on land.**

 Most amphibians are born in water. But some kinds of salamanders and frogs are born on land. They never live in water.

Amphibians in the World

Amphibians around the world help humans in many ways. They eat bugs that harm crops. Their poisons can be turned into medicines. They live in homes as pets. They are even a source of food for some people and animals.

Salamanders eat pesky bugs.

Many amphibians are in danger. People have cut down their forest homes. Rivers, streams, and ponds are polluted. These changes harm amphibians. Some kinds of amphibians have even gone **extinct**. People are working to protect amphibian homes. That way, these animals can stick around for a long time.

Ponds like this need to be kept clean for amphibian homes.

Glossary

bask To lie in the sun to warm up.

carnivore A meat-eating animal.

cold-blooded An animal whose body temperature matches the air around it.

extinct Died out.

gill A body part that an animal such as a fish uses to breathe underwater.

larva A newly-hatched amphibian.

mate To come together to make babies.

mucus A thick, slippery liquid made by an animal.

predator An animal that hunts other animals.

prey An animal that is food for another animal.

Read More

Berger, Melvin and Gilda. *Amphibians*. New York: Scholastic, 2011.

Cleary, Brian P. *Salamander, Frog, and Polliwog: What Is an Amphibian?*. Minneapolis: Millbrook Press, 2013.

Silverman, Buffy. *Do You Know about Amphibians?* Minneapolis: Lerner, 2010.

Websites

Enchanted Learning.com: Amphibian Printouts
http://www.enchantedlearning.com/coloring/amphibians.shtml

NeoK12: Amphibians
http://www.neok12.com/Amphibians.htm

San Diego Zoo: Kids: Amphibians
http://kids.sandiegozoo.org/animals/amphibians

Index

About the Author

Michelle Levine has written and edited many nonfiction books for children. She loves learning about new things—like amphibians—and sharing what she's learned with her readers. She lives in St. Paul, Minnesota.